Look at You, Katie Woo!

by Fran Manushkin

illustrated by Tammie Lyon

PICTURE WINDOW BOOKS
a capstone imprint

Katie Woo is published by Picture Window Books,
A Capstone Imprint
151 Good Counsel Drive, P.O. Box 669
Mankato, Minnesota, 56002
www.capstonepub.com

First published in 2010 by Picture Window Books as:
The Big Lie
Boss of the World
A Nervous Night
No More Teasing

Library of Congress Cataloging-in-Publication data is
available on the Library of Congress website.
ISBN: 978-1-4048-6596-9 (paperback)

Summary: Four stories about Katie Woo, a sweet and sassy school girl.

Photo credits:
Fran Manushkin, pg. 112
Tammie Lyon, pg. 112

Art Director: Kay Fraser
Graphic Designer: Emily Harris
Production Specialist: Michelle Biedscheid

Printed in China.
092010
005924

Katie's Stories

The Big Lie

Table of Contents

Chapter 1
The Missing Plane

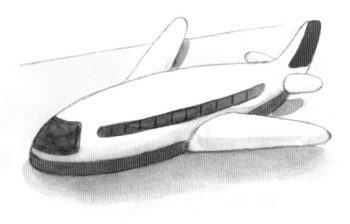

One day after recess,

Miss Winkle told the class,

"Jake has lost his toy airplane.

Has anybody found it?"

Katie Woo
shook her head
no. So did her
friends Pedro
and JoJo and
everyone else.

"My father gave me the airplane yesterday," said Jake.

"It was a birthday

present," he said.

"Maybe your plane flew

away," said someone else.

"That is not funny," said

Miss Winkle.

JoJo told Jake, "I saw you playing with your plane at recess. It's so neat! I hope you find it."

Miss Winkle asked again,

"Does anyone know where

Jake's airplane is?"

"I don't," Katie told Jake.

But she was lying.

Chapter 2

Katie's Bad Grab

Earlier that day during

recess, Katie saw Jake

running around with his

airplane.

"I want to do that!" Katie

told herself. "I wish that

plane belonged to me."

When recess was almost

over, three fire trucks sped by.

While everyone was watching them and waving to the firefighters, Katie grabbed Jake's plane. She put it into her pocket.

Now Jake's plane was

inside Katie's desk.

"I can't wait to play with

it when I go home," Katie

thought.

During art class, Katie said, "Maybe a kangaroo hopped over and put the airplane in her pouch."

"I don't think so," said Miss Winkle. "There are no kangaroos around here."

During spelling, Katie
said, "Maybe the garbage
man came and took Jake's
plane."

"No way!" JoJo said. She
shook her head. "I didn't see
any garbage trucks."

Jake kept staring at the empty box that his airplane came in. The birthday ribbon and paper was still on the box.

Jake looked like he was going to cry.

Katie didn't feel happy
either.

When nobody was
looking, she took something
out of her desk and put it
into her pocket.

Chapter 3

The Truth

Katie walked to the

window and began using

the pencil sharpener.

All of a sudden, Katie

yelled, "I see Jake's plane. It's

by the window! It must have

flown in during recess."

Katie handed Jake the

plane. She whispered, "That

was a lie, Jake. I took your

plane, and I am very sorry!"

At first, Jake was angry at Katie. Then he said, "I am glad you gave it back. I feel a lot better now."

"I do too!" Katie said.

And that was the truth.

Boss of the World

Table of Contents

Chapter 1
Katie Acts Bossy

Katie Woo and her friends

took a trip to the beach.

"Let's do everything

together!" said Katie. "We'll

have so much fun!"

"Let's build the biggest sand castle in the world!" shouted Pedro.

"You two carry the water to me. I will build the castle," said Katie.

"That's not fun!" JoJo said.

"I think it is," replied Katie.

When the castle was

finished, it wasn't very big,

and it kept falling down.

"What a rotten castle!"

Katie moaned.

At lunchtime, Katie

shouted, "I'm so hungry,

I could eat an elephant!"

"Me too!" said JoJo

and Pedro.

They passed French fries

around, but Katie ate most

of them.

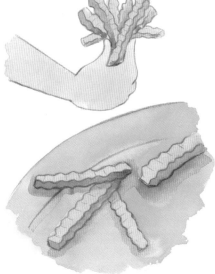

JoJo and Pedro
had only three
fries each.

"I'm still hungry," said
Pedro.

Katie grinned. "I'm not!"
she said.

Chapter 2
Swings and Shells

After lunch, Katie said,

"Let's lie on the blanket. We

can watch the clouds and

kites flying by."

"Katie, move over!" Pedro said. "You are taking up all of the blanket!"

"It's my blanket," Katie said. She did not move one inch. Pedro and JoJo had to lie on the itchy sand.

"Let's go over to the playground," Pedro said. "There are big swings there."

The three friends raced each other. Katie got there first and grabbed the only empty swing.

JoJo and Pedro watched

her swinging for a while.

Then they walked away.

"What's wrong with

them?" Katie wondered.

She ran after

her friends,

saying, "Let's

look for seashells!"

The three friends took

off their shoes. They walked

barefoot along the shore.

The waves tickled their toes.

"I see a giant shell!"
Pedro shouted.

He began running. But he
tripped over some driftwood
and fell down.

Katie grabbed the seashell.

"Hey, that's not fair!"

said JoJo. "Pedro saw the

giant shell first."

"Finders keepers," Katie

insisted.

JoJo and Pedro made

faces and walked away.

Chapter 3
No More Meanie

Katie grabbed her beach

ball and began tossing it

around, but it wasn't any fun.

Just then, JoJo and

Pedro and JoJo's dad began

swimming and splashing

around in the waves.

Katie ran over, shouting,

"I want to swim, too!"

"No!" yelled JoJo. "You

can't! The sea belongs to us!"

"That's silly," Katie said.

She laughed. "The sea can't

belong to you."

"And all the French
fries don't belong to you,"
said Pedro.

"And all the seashells,"
added JoJo.

"And the blankets and
swings," said Pedro.

"Uh-oh!" said Katie
Woo. "I think I have been
a meanie."

"For sure!" said Pedro
and JoJo.

"I'm sorry!" said Katie. "I won't be a meanie anymore. Is it okay if I share the sea with you?"

"Yes!" said her friends.

And there were plenty of waves for everyone!

A Nervous Night

Table of Contents

Chapter 1

A Sleepover

Katie Woo was going to a

sleepover at Grandma and

Grandpa's house.

She packed her suitcase.

Then she kissed her mom

and dad goodbye.

Katie climbed into the car.
"I'm so glad you moved
close to me," she told her
grandparents. "Now I can
sleep over a lot!"

When Katie saw the house, she smiled.

"It's a little house in a big woods," she said.

"It's cozy," said Grandma. "You'll see."

Katie put her suitcase in

the guest room.

It didn't look cozy at all.

The bed was too big, and

the walls were a yucky color.

"Come and plant some tomatoes with me," said Grandpa.

Outside, Katie dug holes and dropped tiny seeds in them.

"In the summer, we'll pick the tomatoes together," Grandpa promised.

Inside, Katie helped Grandma make wontons.

"The next time you visit," said Grandma, "we'll make noodle soup."

"This house is fun," Katie said.

"Indoors and out!" said Grandma. "From our porch we can see the sunset."

"And when you come in the summer," said Grandpa, "you will see shooting stars."

Chapter 2

The High Bed

"It's bath time!" called

Grandma.

"Hey," Katie said, "this

tub has legs. Are you sure it

won't walk away with me?"

"I'm sure," said Grandma.

"You never know," said
Katie.

After her bath, Katie put
on her pajamas.

"I don't like this bed,"

Katie decided. "It's too high.

What if I fall out?"

"This is your mother's old

bed," Grandma said. "She

never fell out."

"Really?" said Katie.

"Being up so high *does* make me feel like a princess."

"And our home is your castle," Grandma said with a smile.

"This castle is a little spooky right now," Katie told Grandpa.

"Don't worry!" he told her. "We have a night-light."

"Yikes!" Katie yelled.

"There's a bear in my castle."

"That's just the shadow of

your mom's old teddy bear!"

said Grandpa.

"Right! I knew that!"

said Katie.

She grabbed the teddy

bear and hugged him tight.

Chapter 3
A Talk with Mom

"Would Princess Katie like some cookies?" offered Grandpa.

"I'd like to call Mom," Katie decided.

"Mom!" said Katie into the phone. "You forgot your teddy bear. Maybe I should come home with it now."

"That's okay," said her mom. "You can bring it back tomorrow."

"Katie," said Grandpa, "I wish you'd stay. I made your favorite — ginger cookies."

"And I will sing your mom's favorite lullabies," Grandma added.

Katie's mom

told her, "Nobody

sings lullabies

like Grandma!

I miss them — and

Grandpa's cookies, too."

"All right!" Katie decided.

"I'll stay."

After cookies and milk,
Katie snuggled under the
covers.

"In the summer," she told
Grandma and Grandpa, "we
will eat tomatoes and make
noodles and see shooting stars!"

"I'm coming back — for sure!" Katie told the teddy bear.

And she dreamed of shooting stars all night.

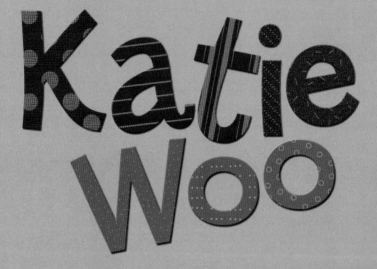

No More Teasing

Table of Contents

Chapter 1
Mean Roddy

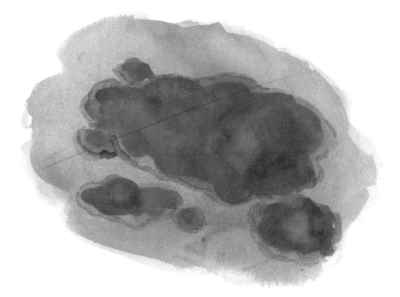

One day, on the way to
school, Katie Woo tripped.
She fell into the mud. Splat!

She scraped her knee, and
mud got on her new sweater
and all of her books.

Katie started

to cry.

"Cry baby! Cry baby!"

yelled Roddy Rogers.

Katie's feelings were so

hurt, she cried harder.

Roddy grinned.

At school, Roddy Rogers

kept teasing Katie during

recess.

"Go away!" she told him.

But Roddy didn't.

At lunch,

they had pizza,

Katie's favorite.

She took such a big bite

that she got tomato sauce on

her nose and cheek.

"Look at Katie," Roddy shouted. "Katie's got a goopy face!"

Roddy said, "Goopy face! Goopy face!"

"Stop it!" cried Katie. But Roddy didn't stop. He was having too much fun.

Roddy made
faces at Katie all
day long.

When Katie stuck

her tongue out at him, he

made more faces. Ugly ones.

"How can I make Roddy

stop teasing me?" Katie

asked her friend JoJo.

But JoJo didn't know.

Chapter 2
The Amazing Butterfly

The next day, Roddy

teased Katie when she was

running at recess. And he

teased her when she was

trying to read her book.

Katie was so unhappy. She
didn't want to go to school
anymore.

The next day, Miss Winkle

told the class, "Everyone,

our butterflies are ready to

hatch. Please hurry over and

watch them!"

Katie pushed up her glasses.

"Hey, I see four eyes!"

Roddy said in a quiet voice.

He knew if Miss Winkle heard

him, he would get in trouble.

Katie was about to

say something back. But

suddenly, her butterfly began

hatching.

It was so amazing. She

couldn't take her eyes off it!

Roddy said, "Four eyes!" a little louder.

But Katie kept watching her butterfly.

Roddy was so mad. He slammed his desk and hurt his finger.

Chapter 3
Stop Teasing!

Later, the class worked

on their "Good Neighbors"

paintings with a partner.

Roddy snuck over to Katie

and said, "Ew! Your painting

is ugly!"

But Katie loved painting so
much that she kept doing it.

"Hey!" Roddy said. "Didn't
you hear me?"

Katie still didn't answer.

Roddy got so mad that he smeared black paint all over his part of his picture.

"Hey!" his partner yelled. "You ruined our painting!"

On the way home, Roddy

glared at Katie, but she

didn't even look at him.

Katie began smiling

and smiling.

When JoJo sat down,

Katie told her, "I'm so happy!

I know how to make Roddy

stop teasing me."

"What do you do?"

asked JoJo.

"Nothing!" Katie said. "When I don't cry or yell, Roddy isn't having fun, so he stops teasing me."

"Katie Woo, you are one smart girl," said JoJo.

"Thanks!" said Katie. And she smiled all the way home.

Having Fun
with
Katie Woo

The Truth and Lies Game

Have you ever told a lie? Has anyone ever lied to you? Everyone knows that lying is wrong. But with the Truth and Lies Game, you can tell lies and nobody will get hurt.

Play this game with a group of friends or classmates.

What you need (one for each player):

• a pen or pencil

• a piece of paper

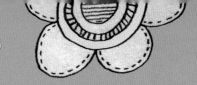

What you do:

1. Each player writes down three items about themselves. You could share your favorite things, best vacations, or hobbies. But one thing should be true and two things should be lies.

2. Take turns reading your lists of three things. After all three items have been read, the group takes a vote on which item is true. When the vote is complete, the reader tells the group which one is true.

You're sure to learn lots of fun things about your friends.

Spot It at the Beach

Katie Woo loves to spend the day at the beach with her friends. Here is a fun game you can play the next time you go to the beach with your pals.

About the Game:

This game asks you to find items that can be seen at the beach. It is like a scavenger hunt, but you do not need to collect the items. Just check the item off your list.

What you need (one for each player):

- a pen
- a piece of paper

What you do:

1. Together, the players make a list of ten or more items to search for. For an extra challenge, make them as detailed as possible.

   Here are some examples:

   - a striped bathing suit

   - a beach ball with three or more colors

   - a towel with a superhero on it

   - a sailboat

2. When your list is done, start searching. Players should mark off the items as they spot them. They should also make a note of where they saw them. The first one to spot all the items on the list wins!

Be a Poet!

How do you feel? Happy? Excited? Sad? Feelings are interesting topics for poems. Try writing an acrostic poem that captures a feeling. In an acrostic poem, the first letters of each line of the poem combine to form a word. That word is the topic of your poem.
So let's get started!

How to Write an Acrostic Poem

1. Choose a feeling word, like happy, angry, or scared. We used the word "nervous" in our example.

2. Write your word going up and down. (See the example at right.) Each letter of the word will become the first letter of each line of your poem.

N
E
R
V
O
U
S

3. Now write the lines of your poem. With each line, describe something that reminds you of your feeling word, like in this nervous poem.

Noises that are creepy

Everyone looking at you

Roller coasters

Visiting the doctor

Owies that bleed

Unfamiliar people

Stormy nights

4. When you are done writing your poem, copy it neatly on a large piece of paper. Then draw pictures that illustrate it. Don't forget to share it with your friends and family!

Partner Pictures

Do you like making pictures? Have you ever made a picture with someone else? It is fun to create art with other people! So grab a partner, and practice working together.

What you need:

- a large piece of poster board. It should be big enough that both of you can gather around it.

- art supplies like pencils, markers, crayons, paints, etc.

What you do:

1. Decide what your picture's theme will be. You should both agree on a theme together.

2. Divide the poster into sections. Each of you will get your own area to work on. You might also want to save a section for words that describe your theme. For example, "Our favorite animals" describes a pet theme.

3. Before you start drawing, talk to your partner about what you will each draw. You might also want to talk about what colors you will use. That way your sections will look nice together.

4. Now start drawing and painting! Before you know it, your teamwork will result in a beautiful picture.

Build a Bird's Nest

Have you ever watched a bird build a nest? Birds use mud, leaves, and grass to make a safe spot for their eggs. With this fun project, you can make a nest of your own.

What you need:

- a brown paper lunch bag

- craft glue

- dried leaves, grass, and flowers

- optional: a bird and eggs from a craft store

What you do:

1. Open up the paper bag. Pull the bottom of the bag up toward the top. As you do this, the sides will crumple. Work with your bag to make it into a bowl shape.

2. Apply some glue to the bag, then stick a leaf on it. Repeat until your bag is covered with leaves. You can also glue on flowers or other lightweight items to decorate your bag.

3. Fill the bag with dried grass. If you would like, add a bird and eggs. Now you have a nest that looks as great as the real thing! Set it on a shelf or table for a pretty decoration.

About the Author

Fran Manushkin is the author of many popular picture books, including *How Mama Brought the Spring; Baby, Come Out!; Latkes and Applesauce: A Hanukkah Story;* and *The Tushy Book.* There is a real Katie Woo — she's Fran's great-niece — but she never gets in half the trouble of the Katie Woo in the books. Fran writes on her beloved Mac computer in New York City, without the help of her two naughty cats, Cookie and Goldy.

About the Illustrator

Tammie Lyon began her love for drawing at a young age while sitting at the kitchen table with her dad. She continued her love of art and eventually attended the Columbus College of Art and Design, where she earned a bachelors degree in fine art. After a brief career as a professional ballet dancer, she decided to devote herself full time to illustration. Today she lives with her husband, Lee, in Cincinnati, Ohio. Her dogs, Gus and Dudley, keep her company as she works in her studio.